A BABY'S GUIDE TO *Surviving* DAD

**Capstone Young Readers**
a capstone imprint

Baby Survival Guides
are published by Capstone Young Readers,
a Capstone imprint
1710 Roe Crest Drive
North Mankato, Minnesota 56003
www.mycapstone.com

Cataloging-in-Publication Data is available on
the Library of Congress website.
ISBN: 978-1-62370-610-4 (Paper Over Board)
ISBN: 978-1-62370-633-3 (eBook)

Printed and bound in China
092015   009224S16

# A BABY'S GUIDE

## TO

## *Surviving*

## DAD

by Benjamin Bird

art by Tiago Americo

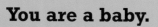

You are a baby.

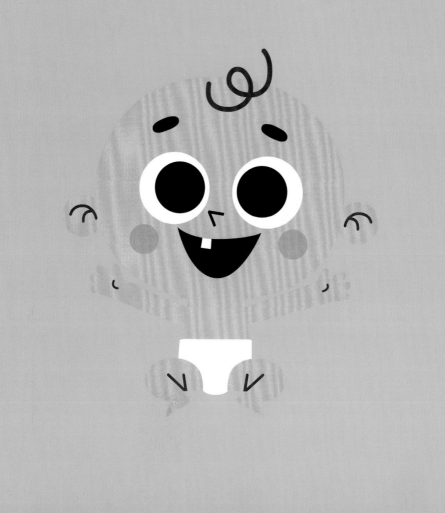

**Like it or not, you need others to survive.**

**Luckily, life gave you a dad.**

So in order to survive, you'll need
to teach him a thing or two.

(Or three. Or four. Or five. Or six . . .)

# Changing Time

When you grow up, people will tell you,
"Practice makes perfect." This is true.

# Give your dad practice.
## Lots and lots of practice . . .

Please refer to
# NUMBER ONE.

# Feeding Time

When you grow up, people might also
tell you, "What goes up, must come down."
This is not true.

**What goes down, must come up.**
**Make sure your dad knows this.**

# Playtime

Playtime is easily confused with Feeding Time.

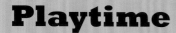

# NOT FOOD

**Teach your dad the difference.
Your survival depends on it.**

# Bath Time

On the other hand, baths are not
necessary for survival. If they were,
why doesn't Dad take one too?

On second thought, maybe he should.

# Sleepy Time

**Lastly, to stay safe at night, one of you should always stand guard.**

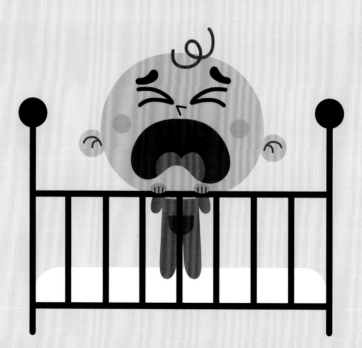

Allow him to take the first watch.
He's older, after all.

**Congrats, baby!**
**Soon you'll be in good hands.**

**And remember . . .**
**you can't survive without Dad.**

**And Dad can't survive
without you.**